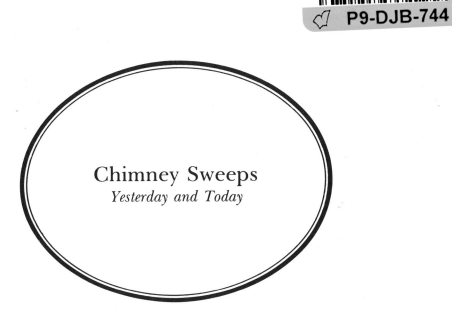

Chimney Sweeps
Yesterday and Today

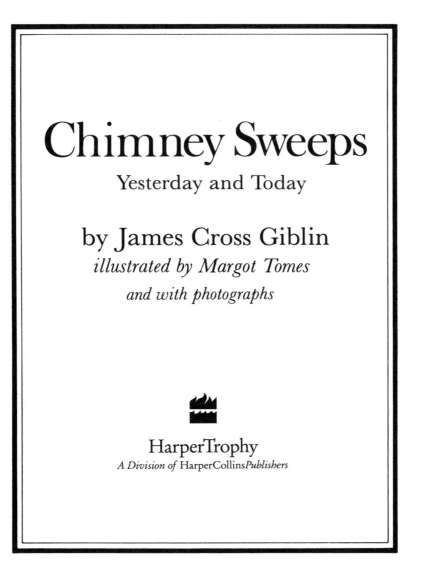

Chimney Sweeps

Yesterday and Today

by James Cross Giblin

illustrated by Margot Tomes
and with photographs

HarperTrophy
A Division of HarperCollins*Publishers*

Acknowledgments

For their help with research for this book, grateful thanks to the following: Sandy Borcherding; Barbara A. Dicks; Goethe House, New York; Handwerkskammer für Mittelfranken, Nuremberg; Ginny Moore Kruse; the Library of Congress; Museum für Deutsche Volkskunde, Berlin; the Economics Division of the New York Public Library; Stella Pevsner; Jeanne Prahl; WCBS-TV, New York.

Special thanks go to Christopher Curtis, master chimney sweep, who gave me the idea for the book and provided valuable information and encouragement throughout its development.

Library of Congress Cataloging in Publication Data
Giblin, James Cross
  Chimney sweeps.

  Bibliography: p.
  Includes index.
  Summary: Traces the history and folklore of the chimney-sweeping profession from the fifteenth century to the present day, emphasizing the plight of the often abused climbing boys of past centuries.
  1. Chimney-sweeps—History—Juvenile literature.
[1. Chimney sweeps] I. Tomes, Margot, ill. II. Title.
HD8039.C48G5 1982   305'.964   81–43878
ISBN 0-690-04192-6   AACR2
ISBN 0-690-04193-4 (lib. bdg.)

  "A Harper Trophy book"
ISBN 0-06-446061-4 (pbk.)

First Harper Trophy edition, 1987

For Davida

Contents

Chimney sweep at work today in Plattsburgh, New York.

Photo by
Christopher Curtis

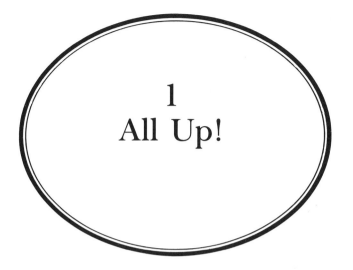

1
All Up!

On a sunny October morning, a van pulls up in front of a ranch-style house in an American suburb. Out jump a young man and woman dressed in black tailcoats and top hats. They are both professional chimney sweeps, and are wearing the costume that has been the trademark of chimney sweeps for almost four hundred years.

While the young woman removes a large vacuum cleaner from the van and wheels it into the house, the young man raises a ladder against the outside wall nearest the chimney. Then, armed with a stiff wire brush and several extension rods, the man climbs the ladder. He is still wearing his top hat. According to chimney sweep superstition, it will keep him from falling off the roof.

After the man gets to the top of the ladder, he crawls up the slanting roof to the chimney. He calls down the chimney to his partner inside the house to make sure she is ready. Then he fastens the brush to the first of the extension rods and lowers it into the chimney to begin the cleaning process.

Down below, the young woman is waiting with the vacuum for the first load of soot to fall. If the chimney hasn't been cleaned in a year or so, the soot may fill the entire vacuum bag.

Before the day is over, these sweeps will clean seven or eight more chimneys in the suburban town where they work. They will take turns climbing the ladder to the roof and operating the vacuum cleaner inside the house.

This is how chimneys are cleaned today, but the job was done very differently in the past. Imagine yourself traveling back in time to a quiet street in London, England, in the year 1800. It is just before dawn, and the chimneys on top of the five-story brick houses are outlined against a pale pink sky.

Suddenly a loud cry breaks the silence. "All up!"

Then the head of a small boy pokes up from the chimney of one of the houses. His face is covered with a knitted cap, with holes for the eyes, nose, and mouth. The cap was once navy blue, but now it is black from chimney soot.

He raises himself higher, and at first it seems that he is wearing a black shirt, too. But it is actually his bare chest, covered with soot like his cap. Even though the October morning is chilly, the boy has removed his shirt because

Sweep with
wire brush
and extension rods.
Photo by Glenn Moody

the fabric might catch on the rough bricks and plaster in the chimney.

Again the boy cries "All up!" to announce to his master below that he has safely reached the chimney top. He happily waves his cleaning tools, a small wire brush and a metal scraper, as he looks out over the rooftops of London. Feeling free, he yanks off his cap and waves it, too, while he takes deep breaths of fresh air.

Then he puts his cap back on and lowers himself into the chimney once more. His work is far from done. Before the day is over, he will have to climb and clean at least eight more chimneys.

2
The First Chimneys

Chimneys didn't come into widespread use until the 1100s. Before then, fires for heating and cooking were built on an open clay hearth in the middle of a room, or in a metal pan called a brazier that was raised above the floor on metal legs. The smoke from these fires escaped through a hole in the roof, or through an open door or window, or sometimes through chinks in the walls.

The first people to build chimneys like those we have today were the Normans, who came from France and conquered England in 1066. The Normans erected great castles and tall houses of two and more stories. A central hearth with a hole in the roof above would not work in such buildings.

At first the Normans laid fires in a shallow recess in the outside wall of a room and hoped the smoke would go out through a hole in the back. Later, in order to get

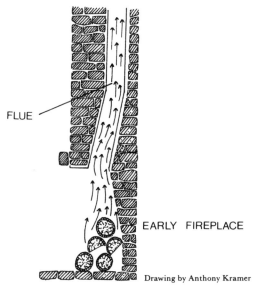

FLUE

EARLY FIREPLACE

Drawing by Anthony Kramer

rid of the smoke more efficiently, they constructed a flue, or shaft, in the outside wall. The flue rose through the wall from the hearth to the roof and carried smoke up and away. Thus the chimney was born.

In the days of the Normans, and for a long time afterward, only the rich had chimneys, for only they could afford to build such elaborate homes. But by the time of England's Queen Elizabeth I, in the late 1500s, chimneys were much more common. A room without its own fireplace was not considered fit for a guest.

Many English houses in the 1600s were built around a central chimney stack. The stack was big enough to carry the flues from four different fireplaces. Large houses might contain as many as six chimney stacks, two at each end of the house and two more in the middle.

Some people put false chimney tops on their roofs to

make their dwellings look more impressive. Most of these were hastily removed, however, when King Charles II decided that chimney stacks were a sign of a person's wealth and levied a tax on them.

The idea of the chimney spread rapidly. The first German chimneys were built about 1350, and by the 1500s chimneys were common features of houses and buildings in France, Italy, and other countries as well as England.

Wherever there were chimneys, they had to be kept clean. Otherwise, not enough oxygen would reach the fire on the hearth, and it would die out. Or else the smoke from the fire would go into the house instead of up the chimney.

Dirty chimneys were also a major cause of fires. Deposits of creosote or coal tar were formed when unburned gases from a wood or coal fire condensed on the inside of a cold chimney. If these deposits weren't removed, they often burst into flame. The walls of the chimney became red-hot, and the fire might spread to the walls, floors, or roof of the building.

In a low-ceilinged country cottage, cleaning the chimney was an easy task. The owner could simply reach up into the chimney with a broom or leafy branch and sweep down the soot and creosote. But that wasn't possible in buildings of several stories, with tall chimneys. Cleaning them was a much more difficult and dangerous job, one that required special skills and daring.

To do the job, a new type of worker soon appeared in the streets of cities all across Europe: the chimney sweep.

3
Chimney Sweeps' Luck

Chimney sweeping became a regular profession in Germany in the 1400s, after German cities passed laws that every homeowner had to have his chimneys cleaned at least twice a year.

German chimney sweeps banded together in a guild and established rules for the profession. Beginning sweeps had to serve a three-year apprenticeship with a master sweep before they could go out to work on their own. In return, master sweeps had to provide apprentices with food, clothing, and a decent place to live.

At the end of their apprenticeship, the new sweeps had to pass a difficult test. While a committee of master sweeps watched, each apprentice had to climb and clean a broad, tall chimney by himself. He was judged on his speed, thoroughness, and cleanliness. If the apprentice sweep let waves of soot blow out into the room while he was cleaning, he was sure to fail the test.

Sweeps first began to wear their traditional uniform of a top hat and black tailcoat in Europe in the 1500s. They often got these clothes secondhand from undertakers. Some say that sweeps chose such formal clothing in order to prove to people that chimney sweeping was a respectable, dignified profession. Others think it was because black clothes didn't show the soot that usually covered the sweeps.

Their black clothes and startling appearance caused many superstitions to grow up around chimney sweeps.

In England in the 1700s, sweeps marched every year in a May Day procession. The leader of the procession was a man dressed as Jack-in-the-Green, an ancient character who represented summer. From head to foot the man was encased in a wicker cage covered with green branches, leaves,

and flowers. Behind Jack-in-the-Green came the sooty-faced sweeps in their black clothes. They represented the dark, dreary days of winter that summer was replacing.

Sweeps became associated in many places with good luck. This was probably because climbing chimneys and roofs was dangerous work; yet most sweeps went about their duties cheerfully, and survived.

It is still considered lucky for a bride to be kissed by a chimney sweep and for a groom to shake a sweep's hand. An old French story tells how this superstition may have come about.

Early one New Year's morning, a young sweep, dressed in the usual top hat and tails, climbed out on the steep roof of a house in Paris. Whistling, he dropped a rope down the chimney and was about to start cleaning it when suddenly he lost his balance. He slipped off the roof head over heels and would have fallen to the street below if his tailcoat hadn't caught on the drainpipe.

A young woman looked out the window of her room and screamed when she saw the handsome young sweep hanging there upside down. He smiled, doffed his hat, and asked her if she would kindly lend him a hand.

Thinking quickly, the woman reached out and pulled the sweep into the room. His tailcoat was torn, but the young woman said she could mend it. The grateful sweep kissed her as the crowd watching below applauded.

In the street the chimney sweep was received like a prince. Everyone wanted to shake the hand of such a lucky man. Later, according to the story, the sweep and the young woman were married.

The account of their love spread far and wide, and people began to believe that a sweep's kiss and handshake would bring good luck to newly married couples. Even today, in England and other countries, sweeps often wait outside churches to kiss a bride's cheek and shake the hand of the groom. Of course, they usually expect to receive a coin or two for their blessing.

A person who meets a sweep and bows to him three times is also supposed to have good luck. According to a story told in England, the first person who experienced this kind of "chimney sweeps' luck" was King George III, who ruled during the 1700s.

One afternoon the King was out riding in a London park when a rabbit ran across the bridle path and frightened his horse. The terrified animal began to buck and rear while the King's companions watched in horror. A chimney sweep who was passing by dropped his brushes and bag of soot when he saw what was happening. He hurried over, grabbed the reins of the King's horse, and managed to calm him down.

If the sweep hadn't come to his rescue, the King might have been thrown from the horse and trampled to death. In gratitude, the King removed his hat and bowed three times to the dirty sweep. All of the King's companions did the same, and soon people everywhere began to link bowing to a sweep with good luck.

4
Climbing
Boys

While superstitions about the luck of chimney sweeps spread, the real lives of sweeps in England became harder and harder in the 1700s.

London and other English cities were growing, and people were building new streets lined with tall, narrow houses. All the rooms in these houses needed fireplaces. But the chimney stack containing the flues from the fireplaces had to take up as little space as possible.

Architects solved this problem by making the flues smaller. Most of those in the new London houses only measured nine inches by fourteen inches. The flues often ran in a zigzag line through the thick walls of a house to the chimney top. People believed that crooked flues would keep more heat inside the house instead of letting it escape straight up the chimney with the smoke.

At the same time flues were getting smaller and more

crooked, more coal was being mined in England. As the supply grew, the price of coal was reduced, and by the late 1700s it replaced wood as the chief heating fuel in England.

All of these changes made it harder to clean chimneys. The soot and creosote from burning logs could easily be swept out of the large older chimneys by servants or chimney sweeps. But the soot from coal fires clung more tightly to the sides of the new, smaller flues and piled up in the corners where the flues made sharp turns.

Adult sweeps were too big to climb up through the narrow flues, and they couldn't get their long-handled brooms around the turns and bends. Only very young boys were small enough to crawl up into the new chimneys and clean out the soot by hand.

These young sweeps were called "climbing boys," and in 1785 it was estimated that there were almost 500 of them in London alone. The boys worked for master sweeps, who were supposed to provide them with food, clothing, and shelter. In 1788, Britain's Parliament passed an act that said climbing boys should be treated as well as any other apprentices. The act also said no children under the age of eight could work as chimney sweeps.

Many master sweeps broke the law, however, and employed children of six, five, and even four years of age. The younger and smaller a child, the more easily he could climb up into the tiny flues, some of which were now only six inches square.

Master sweeps got apprentices from orphanages and sometimes from the children's own parents. In England at the time, there were many poor families with more children than they could afford to feed. Such families were glad to apprentice one of their small sons to a master sweep for five years in return for two or three pounds—about five to eight dollars. The smallest and healthiest boys brought the highest prices.

Some master sweeps did not pay for their apprentices. Instead they kidnapped them from schoolyards and church-yards, or off the streets, and dragged them away to distant parts of the city. It might be years before a kidnapped boy managed to escape and find his way back home again.

If they had children of their own, master sweeps often used them to clean chimneys. Sometimes a master would send one of his little daughters up an especially narrow flue, since girls were usually smaller than boys.

As more masters broke the law and bought or kidnapped little children, English people began to think of chimney sweeps as criminals. They continued to hire master sweeps to clean their chimneys, but they watched with suspicion every move they and their apprentices made while at work in the people's houses.

In Germany at the beginning of the 1800s, few children were employed as sweeps, and most adult chimney sweeps were still treated with respect. In England, however, they were thought to be little better than beggars. They wore hand-me-down clothing and lived in the worst slums. And the sweeps who suffered the most were the youngest—the climbing boys.

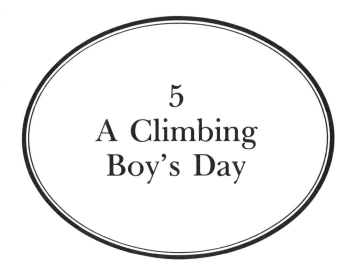

5
A Climbing
Boy's Day

What was it like to be a climbing boy in London in 1800?

To understand that, imagine yourself traveling back in time as we did at the beginning of the book. Then imagine that you are one of three climbing boys working for a master sweep. You are eleven years old and have been cleaning chimneys ever since you were six, when your parents sold you to the master.

It is 4:30 in the morning when the master comes down into the cellar to wake you. You get up every day before dawn because the best time to clean chimneys is in the early morning hours, before people light their fires.

"Get up! Get up!" the master shouts, and the three of you jump up from the burlap bags full of soot that are your only beds. Everyone moves quickly, for you know the master will shake or slap you if you don't.

After stuffing your blanket, which is just a sooty piece of cloth, into an empty burlap bag, you sling the bag over your shoulder. Then you take your cleaning brush and scraper from a shelf above the makeshift beds and follow the master and the other sweeps up the cellar steps.

None of you has to get dressed since you slept in the clothes you wear every day—a tattered jacket over a gray undershirt, and black trousers with patches on the knees. Even though it is October and chilly, the three of you go barefoot; you have to, for you have no shoes. In winter, when it's icy, you tie rags around your feet.

Upstairs, in the single small room where the master lives, his wife serves breakfast: two crusts of bread that you dip in a dish of cold gravy left over from the master's supper the night before.

You don't wash your face or hands before eating. There is no running water in the house, and you and the other climbing boys only bathe on Sunday mornings when you carry pails of water from a public well.

After breakfast you grab your bag, brush, and scraper and follow the master and the other sweeps down the stairs to the street. A young journeyman named John joins you there. John was once an apprentice like you, but now at sixteen he is too big to climb chimneys himself. He lives in an attic room in the lodging house and helps the master train new apprentices.

It is still dark outside, but food sellers along the street are already opening their stalls. The smell of freshly baked

rolls makes you realize how hungry you are. But the master and John hurry all of you along. Today they want to cover a wealthy neighborhood that's a two-mile walk from where you live.

Peter, the youngest apprentice, soon begins to shiver. By the time you turn down a tree-lined street of brick houses, the little boy's teeth are chattering from the cold. John tells him to keep moving if he wants to stay warm.

"Sweeps! Sweeps here! We'll clean your chimney from the bottom to the top!" the master calls in a loud voice.

A maid runs up from the basement of a house farther down the street and waves to the master. "You've come at just the right time," she says. "We were about to start the kitchen fire."

"My boys and I are always out bright and early," the master says with a wink at John.

"How much do you charge?" the maid asks.

"Twelve pence per flue," the master says.

"Oh, that's too much," the maid replies. "We only paid nine pence a flue the last time we had them cleaned."

"How about ten pence?" the master asks. "My boys do a fine job, and I've got a little fellow to climb the smallest flues." He pats Peter on the shoulder, which only makes the boy shiver more.

"Well, I guess that'll be all right," the maid says. "Our chimney's sorely in need of cleaning. Come in. Come in." She motions for the master and the rest to follow her downstairs into the kitchen of the house.

The master and John drape one of your sooty blanket cloths over the fireplace opening. This will prevent soot and dust from coming out into the kitchen. Then the master tells you to get ready to climb the chimney.

You take off your jacket and shirt and put them on the floor. John gives you a stocking cap with small holes for the eyes to pull down over your face. The knitted cap helps to keep soot from getting into your nose.

Grabbing your brush and scraper, you go behind the blanket drape and look up the chimney. At the top you can see a patch of pale blue sky. Good. The chimney flue is straight and quite wide; it shouldn't be too hard to climb.

First you get a foothold on several of the bricks in the chimney wall. Then, bracing yourself with your elbows and your knees, you inch your way upward. When you first started climbing five years ago, your arms and legs were often rubbed raw by the bricks. Gradually they became covered with thick, hard calluses, and now you don't feel the pain as much.

As you climb, you scrape and brush soot from the chimney's walls and from ledges where it has accumulated. The soot falls all around and down to the hearth below. Despite the stocking cap, some of it gets in your eyes, making you blink, and some of it gets in your nose and mouth, too.

At last, twenty minutes after you started climbing, you reach the top of the chimney, fifty feet above the street. "All up!" you shout as you take in great gulps of the cool morning air. Then back down the chimney you climb, scraping and brushing again as you go. You know the master or John will punish you if you dawdle.

Back on the hearth, the other sweeps help you put the fallen soot into one of the burlap sacks. There may be as much as a half bushel. The soot will be carried back to the master's basement and later he'll sell it to farmers for use as fertilizer on their crops.

"Watch that you don't touch anything!" the maid says as she leads you and the other sweeps up the back stairs to the parlor. In it is a fancy fireplace, with a much smaller chimney flue to climb and clean.

The master orders Peter, the youngest apprentice, to climb this one. When the little boy begins to sob, the master turns quickly to Henry, the other sweep, and says, "You'll go up after him to make sure he gets started proper."

Henry nods and leads Peter over to the fireplace, where both boys remove their shirts and put on caps. Peter is still crying, and you know why. You remember what it was like when you were little, and an older sweep, climbing below you, stuck pins in the soles of your feet to make you keep on going when you were afraid.

Henry and Peter disappear behind the dust cloth that hangs over the mantel, and you can hear them begin to climb. "Get on with it!" Henry shouts.

A few minutes later Henry lifts the cloth and comes into the parlor. "Peter's climbin' nice and smooth," he tells the master. "I only had to poke his feet once."

Peter himself reappears about twenty minutes later. He

is black with soot from head to toe, and his elbows and knees show red where they have been scraped by the bricks. But at least he didn't get stuck the way beginners often do. One little boy you worked with got trapped in an especially narrow flue and died from lack of air before he could be rescued.

You and Henry take turns climbing and cleaning the flues in the upstairs bedrooms. They go faster because it's not so far to the roof.

In one room there's a boy about your age, the son of the family that lives in the house. You'd like to talk to him, but he runs away before you have a chance. That's what usually happens with children you meet. Your sooty clothes and face frighten them. Only other climbing boys are able to accept you as you are.

Downstairs again, the maid pays the master for all the flues you and Henry and Peter have climbed. None of you gets any money, but the maid is kinder than some. She gives each of you a hot biscuit just out of the oven and even spreads a bit of butter on top. That's a real treat—it isn't often you taste butter.

"Hurry up, boys!" the master says. He's eager to find more chimneys to clean.

You gulp the rest of your biscuit and sling a bag full of soot over your shoulder. Then you follow the master up the steps and into the street.

"Sweeps! Sweeps here!" John the journeyman calls as you move along.

Before the morning is over, you and the other boys will climb and clean all the flues in two more houses. But that won't be the end of your working day. In the afternoon, after the master has gone home or to his pub, John will lead you and the other sweeps in a search for more chimneys to clean.

The afternoon is the hardest part of the day for you. John makes you work twice as fast because he only gets to keep a small part of what he earns for each flue. The rest he has to give to the master. And often the chimneys you climb are still hot from fires they've had in them earlier in the day.

Once John made you climb a chimney where a fire was blazing in some soot near the top. The higher you went, the hotter it got, and before you finally beat out the flames your face and hands were badly burned.

Luckily, nothing like that happens today and at sundown you trudge home, dragging three bags of soot behind you. Your arms and legs ache, as they do every night, and you're very hungry, and very tired.

Supper, like breakfast, is bread and gravy washed down with a mug of hot tea. "And we have something extra tonight," the master's wife says as she serves up steaming bowls of soup. It's full of leftover vegetables she brought home from the food stall where she works.

"What do you say to that, boys?" the master asks.

"Thank you, ma'am, thank you," you and Henry and Peter reply.

"May I have some more?" Peter asks, and the master's wife refills his bowl halfway. For the first time all day, Peter isn't shivering.

After supper you light a stub of candle and lead the way down into the cellar. It is only 7:30, but everyone is too tired to play or even to talk.

You lie down on the bags of soot you collected during

the day and snuff out the candle. Before long you can hear Henry and little Peter breathing heavily in sleep.

You know you should get to sleep yourself. Soon it will be 4:30 in the morning again, and the master will be calling for you to "Get up and be quick about it!"

But tonight memories of your family fill your mind. Often there wasn't enough to eat, or any wood for the fireplace, but at least you were all together—your father and mother, your brothers and sisters, and you. "Will we ever be together again?" you wonder silently. "Or will I just go on climbing chimneys forever?"

Turning over on the lumpy sack, you make yourself as comfortable as possible and finally fall asleep.

6
Help for
Climbing Boys

While English climbing boys lived through days like the one just described, and thought no one cared about them, some people in London were trying to find ways to help them.

In 1803, a wealthy gentleman became concerned about young sweeps after a climbing boy was caught in his chimney and had to be dug out. With a group of friends, the man formed a society to improve the working conditions of apprentice chimney sweeps. The society hired inspectors to investigate all the master sweeps in the city. The inspectors were supposed to make sure that the law was being obeyed and that no children under the age of eight were employed as climbing boys.

To get a more complete picture of the lives of climbing boys, the society held a series of hearings. They invited master sweeps, climbing boys, and doctors who had treated them to come to the hearings and tell about their experiences.

From their testimony, the society members discovered that most climbing boys suffered from one or more serious ailments. Some boys had badly swollen eyelids or weak sight because they were constantly rubbing soot out of their eyes. Many caught colds, asthma, or tuberculosis from being out in the cold and exposed day after day to dust and soot. Others had crooked spines or deformed arms and legs because they had been made to climb chimneys when their bones were still soft and growing.

Worst of all, many boys were victims of the terrible disease known as "chimney sweeps' cancer." Since weeks often went by between washings, soot would accumulate in the boys' crotches and irritate the skin. Instead of healing, these sores sometimes hardened into cancerous lumps. If the lumps weren't discovered and removed in time, the boys might die.

The society members learned that only one climbing boy in ten knew how to read or write. A few were taken to Sunday school by their masters, but none could go to regular school because they were busy cleaning chimneys in the morning. Besides, few schools wanted the dirty, shabby climbing boys as pupils.

When the boys reached the age of twelve or thirteen and got too big to climb chimneys, most of them were not fit for any other work. Some older boys helped their former masters train apprentices and later became master sweeps themselves. A few went to sea as sailors. Some were so sick and deformed they could only wander the streets as beggars. Others turned to crime.

After hearing all the testimony, the society decided that no children of any age should be forced to work as chimney sweeps. But what could replace them? The answer had to be some kind of machine.

The society offered a prize of 40 guineas (about $200 today) to the person who could invent a successful chimney-sweeping machine. The winning design was submitted by a man named George Smart and featured a round brush large enough to rub against all four sides of a nine-by-fourteen-inch flue. The brush was attached to the top of a short, hollow stick.

As the brush was thrust up the chimney, more sticks were added to the first, each fitting neatly into the one above it. Finally the brush reached the chimney top. Then it was worked down again slowly so that the flue got a double cleaning.

The society had the device tested and an architect reported that three-quarters of the chimneys in London could be cleaned with it. The rest of the chimneys could easily be altered so that the special brushes could be used in them, too.

The results encouraged the society to take its case to the highest levels of English government. In 1804, its supporters offered Parliament a bill urging that the use of climbing boys be outlawed. The bill listed all the evidence the society had gathered about the cruel conditions in which

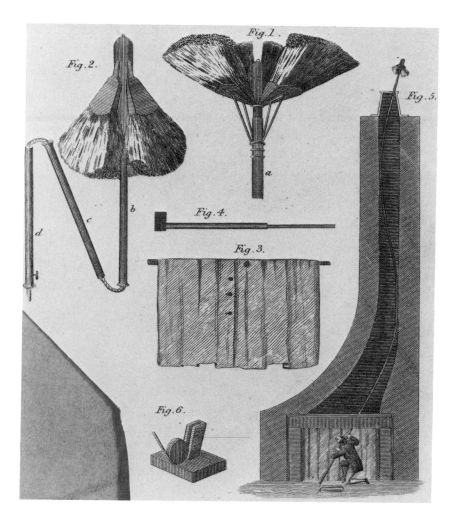

The parts of George Smart's chimney cleaning machine from a 19th century engraving. Cooper-Hewitt Museum, the Smithsonian Institution

the boys lived and worked. Then it described the new cleaning device and explained how it could replace the boys.

The bill met with strong opposition. Master sweeps feared that they would no longer be able to earn a living if others learned to operate the cleaning device. And home-owners feared that the device would be more expensive than climbing boys, especially if their chimneys had to be rebuilt to accommodate it.

Parliament listened to these arguments, and the bill was defeated. But the society did not give up. It gathered more evidence and introduced new bills in Parliament in 1817 and again in 1819.

At the same time, people began protesting other kinds of child labor in England. New factories, mines, and mills were springing up all over the country, and children were being hired to work in them at low wages. In 1816, the reformer and educator Robert Owen proposed that only children above the age of twelve be employed in textile mills and that they work no more than ten hours a day. His suggestions were ignored by the mill owners, but more and more people came to believe that child labor was wrong.

In 1833, Parliament finally passed a bill prohibiting the employment of children under the age of nine in mills and factories. That bill limited the working hours of children ages nine to twelve to eight per day and those of young people ages thirteen to eighteen to sixty-nine per week. The same law raised the minimum age for apprentice climbing boys from eight to ten. And it required that all chimneys in England be altered so that they could be cleaned with extension poles and brushes.

These were important steps forward, but the society still was not satisfied. It continued to press in Parliament for more laws to protect climbing boys. Famous authors like Charles Dickens joined in the fight by writing about the hard life of chimney sweeps in *Oliver Twist* and other books. At last, in 1840, a bill was passed forbidding young men under the age of twenty-one to climb and clean flues as a profession.

The society's struggle wasn't over yet, however. Despite the new laws, master sweeps kept on using children as climbing boys, and there weren't enough policemen or inspectors to stop them. It wasn't until 1875 that Parliament established strict regulations for the licensing of chimney sweeps. When they applied for a license, all master sweeps had to list the names and ages of their apprentices. No longer could they employ small children in secret.

At last the society could relax. For this law finally ended the use of climbing boys in England—a practice that had injured or killed hundreds of children each year for more than a century.

7
Chimney Sweeps in America

When North America was settled in the 1600s and 1700s, the colonists brought along with them the chimney cleaning methods of their native countries.

Farmers in England and Europe often used live geese as chimney sweeps, and many American colonists did also. A settler would climb up onto the roof of his one-story cabin or house and drop a large goose with a rope tied loosely around its feet down the flue. He raised and lowered the goose several times, and trusted that its flapping wings would remove most of the soot from the chimney. Then he gave the dirty, frightened bird a bath.

Other colonists set fire to their chimneys on rainy days to clean them out, but this could be risky. Sometimes sparks flew up and landed on the roof of the house, or on a neighboring building. Because of the danger of fire, many eastern

cities passed laws forbidding this practice. In Philadelphia, if anyone set fire to his chimney to burn out the soot and sparks or flames emerged from the top, he had to pay a fine of twenty shillings—about five dollars.

As American cities grew during the 1700s and there were more chimneys to clean, chimney sweeping became a profession as it was in England. Some American towns appointed official chimney sweeps for their communities, and large cities like Boston had many master sweeps.

American sweeps used a variety of cleaning methods, depending on the size and shape of the chimney. If a flue was fairly wide and not too high, the sweep might simply stand on a ladder and broom it out.

If it was wide but had a turn or two, he would probably crawl up through it, brush and scraper in hand, like the English climbing boys.

If the flue was too narrow for that, he would climb up on the roof and drop a canvas bag filled with bricks down through the chimney on a rope. By raising and lowering the bag, he loosened most of the soot from the chimney walls. The soot fell to the hearth, where it piled up behind a blanket or cloth the sweep had pinned over the mantel.

Rates for cleaning chimneys varied from town to town. In Salem, Massachusetts, the official sweep charged twenty-five cents to clean a one-story flue, forty cents for a two-story flue, and fifty cents for one that was three stories high.

Benjamin Franklin spoke for many American homeowners when he urged that chimney sweeps be regulated carefully. "Those who undertake the sweeping of chimneys," Franklin wrote, "ought to be licensed by the Mayor; and if any chimney fires and flames fifteen days after sweeping, a fine should be paid by the sweeper, for it is his fault."

The city fathers in Philadelphia listened to Franklin and in 1787 enacted a set of regulations for chimney sweeps. Each master sweep was required to clean a flue within forty-eight hours of being called, or pay a fine of five dollars. And if the flue caught fire within a month after it had been swept, the master had to pay a ten-dollar fine.

American master sweeps, like those in England, often took on young apprentices to help them with their work. But the boys were usually treated better than the English climbing boys.

In Baltimore in 1792, master sweep John Zollikoffer placed an ad in a newspaper. He invited parents of large families to apprentice one or two of their sons to him. The boys should be between the ages of eight and ten, and willing to work as chimney sweeps until the age of fifteen, when they would be too big to climb chimneys. At that time Zollikoffer—unlike many masters—promised to help the boys find other means of making a living. The ad ended by saying that only "good-natured and honest boys should apply."

Some cities passed laws about the treatment of apprentice sweeps. In New York City, a master sweep could hire as many apprentices over the age of eleven as he needed, if he applied for a license and paid a fee of three dollars. But, in order to keep the license, the master had to provide the boys with adequate clothing, nourishing food, and comfortable beds. And he couldn't make them work longer than from 6:00 in the morning to 6:00 in the evening.

Despite laws like these, there were some cruel masters in pioneer America. Young black chimney sweeps received the worst treatment. In the South, plantation owners often sent out slave boys to clean their neighbors' chimneys for a fee. If the boys didn't turn over all the money they earned, the owners had them whipped.

Sometimes older slave sweeps, like other blacks, ran away from their masters and obtained forged passes stating that they were free Negroes. Many of them fled to the North, where they settled in cities and took up their old trade as chimney sweeps.

In the early 1800s, the chants of black chimney sweeps could be heard in the streets of New York, Philadelphia, Hartford, and other northern cities:

> *Sweep for your soot, ho,*
> *I am the man,*
> *That your chimney will clean,*
> *If anyone can,*
> *Sweep, ho!*

Like chimney sweeps in Germany and England, the black sweeps usually wore a tailcoat, striped trousers, and a battered top hat. And they were usually followed by two or three small boys who did the climbing.

White boys sometimes ran through the streets after the

black boys. They pointed fingers at their sooty clothes, called them by the nickname "lily white," and laughed at them. More often than not, this made the black sweeps angry, and often there were fights. But, as one black master sweep said. "The people who laughs at us is crazy. I make more money in a day sweeping chimneys than some people who laughs at us make in a week."

No national society like the one in England was ever formed in the United States to fight for the rights of chimney sweeps. However, in 1818, a Quaker group in Philadelphia imported a number of the English cleaning machines. A spokesman for the Quakers said, "We take pleasure in the introduction of the machines here. Perhaps they will remove from chimney sweeping . . . those unfortunate black children who travel our streets in tattered garments during the most severe winter weather."

Although individual cities had regulations, no state or federal laws were ever passed to protect American chimney sweeps either. Their treatment depended on the attitude of people in the places where they lived and worked.

In the upper Midwest, which was settled in the mid-1800s by people from Germany and Sweden, chimney sweeps were treated with the same respect they had always received in those countries.

In San Francisco in the 1880s and 1890s, sweeps were regarded as entertainers. They wore a special costume—red overalls and matching red stocking caps, with bells jingling on top. When they walked through the streets of the city singing their songs, people applauded.

As America left the nineteenth century and entered the twentieth, the cries of chimney sweeps were heard less and less often. By then basement furnaces had replaced fireplaces and stoves as the main source of heat in many American homes and public buildings. Furnaces did not produce as much soot as fireplaces, so chimneys did not have to be cleaned as often. Faced with a decline in business, many chimney sweeps turned to other professions.

By the middle of the twentieth century, it was hard to recognize those chimney sweeps who remained on the job. Most of them now wore white uniforms like gas station attendants. They didn't even call themselves chimney sweeps; instead they were "fluonomists," or technological sweepers. They drove around in trucks equipped with special vacuum cleaners that were designed to clean the dirt from chimney flues and air-conditioning vents. Most of the homes and buildings they serviced were no longer heated with coal, but with fuel oil and natural gas.

Then came the worldwide energy crisis of the 1970s. Alarmed by the rising cost and scarcity of fuel oil, more and more people began to heat their homes with coal- and wood-burning stoves and fireplaces. Once again deposits of soot and creosote formed on the walls of their chimneys and had to be removed.

People who still relied on furnaces wanted their chimneys cleaned more often, too, in order to increase efficiency and reduce the amount of fuel oil that was consumed.

Chimney Sweeps in America

All across the U.S. and around the world, a fresh demand for chimney sweeps arose. To meet it, a new kind of sweep, dressed in the tailcoat and top hat of old, began to appear everywhere.

8
Chimney Sweeps
Today

In France, Sweden, and other European countries, chimney sweeping today is a government service, like snow removal. In these countries, it's the law that all chimneys must be swept at least once a year.

In Germany, sweeps are not just cleaners; they are monitors of the environment. A German sweep is assigned a particular area in a city or town and makes monthly inspections to see whether the homes and factories in his territory are burning fuel efficiently. If the sweep discovers that pollution is occurring, he gives the owner of the building six weeks to remove the cause. If pollution continues after that, the owner has to pay a stiff fine.

Today in the United States, more than 25 million fireplaces and 5 million wood stoves are being used to heat homes. Fireplaces and stoves produce a satisfying and rela-

Dressed in traditional costumes, these men and women were photographed during the 1979 convention of the National Chimney Sweeps Guild in Chicago. Two children appear in the picture also, but they are not working sweeps.

Photo by
Christopher Curtis

tively inexpensive warmth, but they can also be dangerous if chimneys are not kept clean. In 1979, there were 40,000 fires nationwide that could be traced to dirty chimneys. These fires caused $23 million in property damage.

To help reduce the number of fires, over 3000 chimney sweeps are now at work all across the United States. Seminars to train new sweeps are held by manufacturers of chimney-sweeping equipment, and a national organization, the Chimney Sweeps' Guild, has been formed to establish rules and standards for the profession.

Some sweeps clean chimneys full time, but most do it in their spare time while holding down another job. Teachers, actors, college students—all may be part-time chimney sweeps today. The busiest time of the year for sweeps is the fall, when people are getting their fireplaces and stoves ready for winter fires.

Women as well as men sweep chimneys. In the Chicago area, as many as 20 percent of the active chimney sweeps are women. Some work with their husbands, some are teamed with other women or men, and some operate alone.

Both men and women sweeps wear the traditional top hat and tailcoat when they're traveling between jobs or cleaning from the roof. This age-old costume makes them look colorful and also serves as an effective advertisement. People can't help noticing and talking about them. When they're cleaning from inside a house, sweeps generally work in a black T-shirt and trousers.

Many different kinds of protective clothing are also avail-

*Sweep unloading
his portable vacuum cleaner
from a van.*
Photo by Glenn Moody

*A sweep prepares
to clean a chimney
from inside the house.*
Photo by Glenn Moody

able to modern chimney sweeps. Respirators attached to rubber face masks allow sweeps to breathe normally even while working in a fireplace. Leather gloves with long gauntlets enable them to reach deep into stoves or up chimneys without getting their hands and arms dirty. Ski goggles keep dust and soot out of their eyes. No one is cleaning chimneys bare-chested, with only a dirty stocking cap to protect his face, like the English and American climbing boys of the past.

Chimney cleaning methods today aren't so very different from those of the past, however. Modern sweeps usually use stiff wire brushes, many of which are square-shaped so they will reach into the corners of a chimney flue. The brushes are raised and lowered through the chimney on Fiberglas extension rods, much like those used in nineteenth-century chimney-sweeping machines.

One of the most difficult parts of chimney sweeping is keeping the house clean. Most sweeps today use a portable, high-powered vacuum cleaner with a long hose that sucks in the dust before it can drift out of the fireplace and into the room.

Chimney sweeping can still be a hazardous occupation. Sweeps sometimes fall from roofs and break bones. They may be bitten by animals like rats, snakes, or raccoons that occasionally live in chimneys. And constant exposure to dust and soot can be harmful to their eyes and lungs.

But chimney sweeping has its attractive side, too. Sweeps are usually their own bosses, they can set their own working

A sweep takes a chance, and jumps from the top of a chimney to the roof below.

Photo by
Christopher Curtis

Present-day su
atop a chimne
Photo by
Christopher Curti

hours, and they meet many different kinds of people. Modern sweeps charge between $40 and $60 to clean a typical fireplace, which takes about an hour. Sweeps can make as much as $400 a day if they work at the job full-time.

For almost 900 years, chimneys have been an essential part of homes and public buildings, and chimney sweeps have been needed to keep them clean. Chimney sweeps will continue to be needed as long as people use fireplaces and stoves for heating.

When people see a chimney sweep, dressed in top hat and tailcoat, they may be reminded of the sad history of climbing boys. Or perhaps they will remember the stories about chimney sweeps' luck, and will bow to the sweep three times in hopes of getting some of that luck for themselves.

The Chimney Sweeper

by William Blake

When my mother died I was very young,
And my father sold me while yet my tongue
Could scarcely cry " 'weep! 'weep! 'weep! 'weep!''
So your chimneys I sweep & in soot I sleep.

There's little Tom Dacre, who cried when his head
That curl'd like a lamb's back, was shav'd, so I said,
"Hush, Tom! never mind it, for when your head's bare,
You know that the soot cannot spoil your white hair.''

And so he was quiet, & that very night,
As Tom was a-sleeping he had such a sight!
That thousands of sweepers, Dick, Joe, Ned, & Jack,
Were all of them lock'd up in coffins of black;

The Chimney Sweeper

And by came an Angel who had a bright key,
And he open'd the coffins & set them all free;
Then down a green plain, leaping, laughing they run,
And wash in a river and shine in the Sun;

Then naked & white, all their bags left behind,
They rise upon clouds, and sport in the wind.
And the Angel told Tom, if he'd be a good boy,
He'd have God for his father & never want joy.

And so Tom awoke; and we rose in the dark
And got with our bags & our brushes to work.
Tho' the morning was cold, Tom was happy & warm;
So if all do their duty, they need not fear harm.

(from **Songs of Innocence,** *1789*)

Bibliography

Blake, William. *A Selection of Poems and Letters.* Edited by J. Bronowski. New York: Penguin Books, 1958.

"A Copy of the Report presented to the House of Commons by the Committee appointed to examine the several petitions which have been presented to the House against the employment of boys in sweeping of chimneys." London: *The Pamphleteer,* 1817.

Curtis, Christopher, and Post, Donald. *Be Your Own Chimney Sweep.* Charlotte, Vermont: Garden Way Publishing, 1979.

———— *Chimney and Stove Cleaning.* Charlotte, Vermont: Garden Way Publishing, 1977.

Dickens, Charles. *Oliver Twist.* New York: Pocket Books, 1975.

Fletcher, Valentine. *Chimney Pots and Stacks.* London: Centaur Press, Ltd., 1968.

Bibliography

Hoffman-Krayer, Eduard. *Handwoerterbuch des deutschen Aberglaubens.* Berlin, Leipzig, 1931–32.

Hole, Christina. *British Folk Customs.* London: Hutchinson, 1976.

Hudson, John Corrie. "A Letter to the Mistresses of Families on the Cruelty of Employing Children in the Odious, Dangerous, and Often Fatal Task of Sweeping Chimnies [sic], and on the Facility with which the Practice May be Almost Wholly Abolished." London: *The Pamphleteer,* 1823.

Klapper, Joseph. *Schlesische Volkskunde.* Stuttgart: Brentano, 1952.

Montgomery, James. *The Chimney-Sweeper's Friend.* London: Longman, Hurst, Rees, Orme, Brown, and Green, 1824.

Phillips, George L. *American Chimney Sweeps: An Historical Account of a Once-Important Trade.* Trenton, N J : Past Times Press, 1957.

———— *England's Climbing-Boys: A History of the Long Struggle to Abolish Child Labor in Chimneysweeping.* Boston, Mass.: Harvard Graduate School of Business Administration; Baker Library; Kress Library of Business and Economics; Publication #5, 1949.

Quennell, Peter, editor. *Mayhew's London.* London: William Kimber, 1951.

Radford, E., and Radford, M. A. *Encyclopedia of Superstitions.* New York: The Philosophical Library, 1949.

"Report of the Surveyor General of the Board of Works, of the Experiments Made for the purpose of ascertaining the practicability of superseding the necessity of employing climbing boys in the sweeping of chimnies [sic], by means of the employment of machinery." London: Works and Public Buildings Office, 1819.

Shuffrey, L. A. *The English Fireplace.* London: B. T. Batsford, 1912.

Index